The Russian Coup
and the Girl

KIRA VON KORFF

BALBOA.
PRESS
A DIVISION OF HAY HOUSE

Balboa Press books may be ordered through booksellers or by contacting:

Balboa Press
A Division of Hay House
1663 Liberty Drive
Bloomington, IN 47403
www.balboapress.com
1-(877) 407-4847

This is a work of fiction. All of the characters, names, incidents, organizations, and dialogue in this novel are either the products of the author's imagination or are used fictitiously.

ISBN: 978-1-4525-4746-6 (sc)
ISBN: 978-1-4525-4747-3 (e)

Library of Congress Control Number: 2012934479

Printed in the United States of America

Balboa Press rev. date: 3/5/2012

Prologue

It was a warm summer day in Russia, and the birch trees in the forest were swaying and sparkling in the wind. The daffodils were in full blossom. The tanks were rolling, and the snipers were shooting. It was a coup.

I did not want to be inside the hotel, the Radisson-Slavyanskaya, because I was afraid. There were snipers on the roof of the hotel, which was just two blocks away from the White House. Outside, foreigners were watching, oblivious to the danger. They were just spectators looking for a show.

I ran two blocks from the hotel to stand underneath a bridge made of stone, with an arch underneath for people to walk through. It was a very old bridge, dating from before the revolution. There I saw a river across from the White House.

Under the bridge, I was alone but could see everything. Then four men also went under the bridge. They were not young, but they were not old. They were laughing and somber at the same time, dressed in the look of the day: Levi's blue jeans and button-up shirts. They knew what was going on but really did not care.

While the coup was taking place, some things were in disarray. The four men had found a kiosk (common on the streets those days), and they broke into the window and took vodka. They brought the vodka under the bridge and started to drink. I was twenty-one at the time. They told me I was safe.

Otherwise, nothing was affected. The stores had bread, and people still went to work.

Chapter 1

I grew up in a Russian household. My great-grandfather was a baron, and my great-grandmother was a baroness. My great-grandfather was also a general in the tsar's army. I would later see his portrait hanging in the Hermitage Museum. My great-grandmother (Baba) was beautiful and was well respected everywhere she went.

I often remember visiting them in San Francisco, in the cold summer fog, right across from Golden Gate Park. I also remember my grandfather would sit with me, teaching me how to play the piano. He used to put me on his lap, and we would play simple Russian folk songs.

Dinner was oxtail soup and kasha (buckwheat grain) with sour cream. It was delicious. For dessert there was always halva (a paste made from various nuts like pistachio or walnut), which was slightly sweet. We would also go for ice cream and a good walk.

Then we played cards. We played canasta, which is a very old and difficult Russian card game. I was only five at the time, so my mother would lean over and help me with my cards. There were always sweets on the table. There was baklava (my great-grandmother's favorite), chocolates, and halva. We would play for hours.

My great-grandmother had a little white poodle. I will never forget him. He would always greet me at the front door of the San Francisco apartment and run up the stairs with me to the living area. I used to sit at the corner in the hallway, where there was a lamp, table, and chair. I do not know why, but I just liked sitting there.

How did my great-grandmother happen to live in San Francisco? During the Russian Revolution, my great-grandfather transferred them to Shanghai and then to San Francisco. He would later go back to Russia and fight for the tsar. He was eventually killed, and he will always be a hero in my mind for his integrity and keeping his family safe.

Then there was Deeyeda, my uncle. He stayed with Baba until the end. But actually, he was in love with Baba's sister, Olga, who was a famous opera singer. Later, Deeyeda did marry Baba, and he loved her very much.

My grandfather was an admiral in the tsar's army and a close friend of the tsar. I can remember as a child seeing pictures of them together. Although my aunt has those pictures, they belong to the Russian people. They are part of Russian history.

My grandfather taught me how to play the piano. He would dance the old Russian men's folk dance of kneeling and kicking your legs straight up in the air. It was a main event, and everyone clapped to the music and his dancing. He was an athlete; you would have to be to dance this dance! He later joined the US National Guard and then the US Army. My great-grandfather would have been proud.

Chapter 2

It all began with a knock on my door one afternoon. I rented a room in a beautiful, white, Colonial-style house near a university in Washington, DC. It was Denis at the door. He asked, "Are you Kira?" I said yes. He said, "Hello, my name is Denis [which he pronounced Deneese], and I have a postcard from Ed, asking me to contact you."

Denis was short, with striking blue eyes and short blond hair. He was clearly Russian. As I was only a block away from the Russian embassy, where he lived with his family, it was easy for him to deliver the postcard from Ed, a college friend. I liked him and invited him into the house. We had a fine discussion.

He brought me Russian black rye bread and vodka. I learned how to drink the vodka with the bread. "Here we go. Try this," he said.

I invited him to join my friends' social gatherings, and he enjoyed all of it. But he was Russian, and it was not the same as being with Russians in Russia—as I would later find out.

With one of my girlfriends' help, I even found him a job. It was not easy, as he was not officially allowed to work in the United States. He saved his money and would use it to buy a Russian military jeep when we went back to Moscow.

In Washington, DC, it was swelteringly hot. Denis had found a friend in the Russian embassy who knew about cars. He had invited me to Russia with his family, and the sale of my broken-down car would pay for the airline ticket.

Ivan came from the Russian Embassy and fixed my car, an old Volvo. When he came to work on my car, I would always serve him iced tea, as it was so hot during the summertime. Once my car was fixed, it sold for a thousand dollars. At that time, the ticket to fly on Aeroflot, the Russian airline, was $400.00. I had the money to go.

Ivan told Denis he wanted to marry me. He would come into my room, and we would have many discussions. I ignored his marriage proposal as if it never happened. I was young, and marriage was the furthest thing from my mind.

Denis used to tell many jokes. In one of them, a tall man was walking down a sidewalk in Moscow. All of a sudden, a sparrow started to hop right next to him. "I am an eagle, I am an eagle!" the sparrow cried. "Then why are you so small?" the man asked. The sparrow said, "I was ill, I was ill!" Russian jokes usually play on the Russian language. If one knows this, the joke is very funny. Denis was very good at this language-altering and wordplay.

I began to pack for my trip to Russia. As I did not own much, it fit into two pieces of luggage. Denis told me, "You packed well. But do not forget your army boots. They will be a big hit in Russia!" I wore boots from the army store, as they helped my legs for dancing. Second of all, I did not want to be an outsider, so I bought new shoes. But they would not, of course, be appropriate for the Russian winter.

Then it was time to say good-bye to everyone. I also called my mother and gave her Denis's telephone number in Russia.

We went to the airport. Denis, his father, and I were put in the lounge. His father was really very important. Then we boarded the plane on the runway, not from the airline lounge. I had no fear, as I was young. And, of course, I had no idea what to expect. But again, I was young.

"It will be a rough flight," Denis told me. "But really, you will not notice." We were flying on a Russian airplane, and they moved quite a bit in flight, from side to side and up and down. It really did not matter, though, as everyone was served vodka.

Denis pushed the two airline seats in front of him and propped up his legs. I tried to fall asleep. "Well, what am I going to do with you?" he asked me. I was just sitting there, trying to sleep. In those days, I did not drink vodka. However, I did on that plane ride. You just needed it!

The plane landed. The view through the window was stark and white with snow. I left the plane, and a landscape of snow met me in the middle of the day. It showed a low, white sky and, in the background, sparse birch trees that had lost their leaves.

I was twenty-one, and suddenly I was in Russia.

I was deplaned and immediately knew I was home. The cement below my feet felt familiar, as if I had always been there.

We were greeted by Denis' girlfriend and all his friends. "See, that is what a girl should look like!" he said. His girlfriend had lightly curled hair, a lot of makeup, and wore a pretty outfit. The American girls he had met did not wear any makeup. I felt ugly compared to her. But I would soon learn.

"Let's go," Denis said. We got into an old military vehicle and drove to Denis's home in Moscow. Along the way, his girlfriend and friends asked him so many questions. It was a happy occasion. He had been gone two years, living in the Russian Embassy in the United States.

The minute we got home, Denis said, "Here is a cup of tea." It was good, slightly sweet, and very strong. It warmed me from the outside snow.

We talked together for hours. Denis told me about a street I could walk down near his family's apartment. "It is beautiful at dusk," he said. And he was right.

When the party was over, Denis told me, "I am going to walk my girlfriend home [she only lived three blocks away] and then I will show you your bedroom."

His friends left, and I waited for Denis to come back home. I was not tired in the least, and I drank more tea. The tea was good.

Denise returned. "Here is your bedroom," he told me. It was his sister's bedroom and was off the living room. It was small: practically a closet. But I was happy. It had a nice, comfortable bed and pictures on the walls. There was no other room for furniture.

I had no trouble falling asleep. His mother had cooked a very nice dinner. We had stewed beef, pickled beets, and Russian black rye bread. We also had soup, although I did not quite know what was in it. But the meal was good and warm, perfect for winter, and my fullness made me sleepy.

I would grow to love his family's apartment near the street lined with birch trees.

I would often walk in the evening. It was serene, and the snow sparkled in the glow from the street lamps in the winter. In the spring and summer, it was just a tree-lined sidewalk with cascading leaves.

When I returned home, Denis would always say to me, "You are back!" And we would drink tea. It was a routine I looked forward to.

But I knew I needed a job. After two weeks, my money had run out, and I could not depend on Denis. That would not have been appropriate.

We would be friends for many years. He took care of me in Russia. He found me places to live and my first job. Later, after I left, he was in a car accident and was paralyzed. I will always love him.

Chapter 3

After I had lived in Denis's family's Moscow apartment for two weeks, his father and mother had to move to Switzerland.

On my third day in Russia, Denis invited me to a birthday party. In Russia, the person whose birthday it is makes his or her own party. And it is really an extravagant and very happy affair. There is piano music played by the host and singing.

It was beyond even a dream. All the guests brought flower arrangements, as is the custom in Russia. If you bring any kind of food or drink, it is an insult to the host or hostess

The food was spread out in the kitchen and living area. Everything was homemade. It was Alex's (Alexei) birthday, and his mother and father made the food. They were, in their time, famous stage actors. And they were very good Russian cooks.

There were fish and meat pies and stuffed cabbage. There were five different salads, including ones with beets, carrots, and potatoes and peas. There were radishes you dipped in butter and salt; they were very delicious. And, of course, there was caviar and white bread and butter, which is the traditional way to eat caviar in Russia. It was black beluga caviar: the best there is.

Then there were the hot courses. There was meat-stuffed cabbage and stewed mushrooms stuffed with cheese and sour cream. They are the most delicious.

And, of course, there was vodka. The party lasted for hours, so there were many toasts given. Many sang old Russian folk songs, with Alex's father on the piano.

After the party, we all took an evening walk. I felt right at home.

After two years in Russia, I threw my own birthday party. I made apple-stuffed rabbit with buckwheat kasha (grains that are boiled—for example, oats).

I had a hot vegetable dish of cabbage stewed in milk, made with a bay leaf and quite a bit of pepper. There were two salads and caviar on halved hard-boiled eggs.

The party took place at my boyfriend Dima's family's country house, twenty minutes outside of Moscow. It was October, and there was a chill in the air. We all went for a walk on the dirt roads and sang folk songs in the cold October air. We stayed up until at least one o'clock in the morning. It was a good party.

I did leave the party for a half an hour or so. I went and sat behind some birch logs to keep away from the wind. I was alone. The bright night sky was full of stars, and I just sat and pondered about Dima and me. We were not meant to last.

I should mention that it is difficult to throw a party in the average Russian dacha. You wash everything by hand; you have to bring water up to the dacha from the well. Then you have to heat it on the hearth.

But I will never forget it.

Chapter 4

My first job was at the American Science Council. They published a monthly journal, and I was an editor. The council had several rooms in an old stone building. The building was practically vacant and very cold. It was surrounded by leafless birch and fir trees that stood out against the low, white winter sky.

Twelve Americans worked there. Many would joke and laugh. I did not. I was an outsider. I worked alone and then went home. No one really talked to me. They were all friends from the United States, young, and looking for adventure.

I would go by subway to work in the cold, still morning and leave in the afternoon. Russian mornings bring a somber blue sky. And it is so quiet outside.

I was paid a hundred dollars a month. It was more than I needed, as the cost of living in Russia was very low at the time. I was still living with Denis, so I had no rent to pay. But it was not enough money for a fur coat. After three months, I gave my notice and quit. I did not belong there.

One winter day, Denis, his friends, and I had a picnic! We grilled meat and had tomatoes and cucumbers slices. I played fetch with his dog, a pit bull that was so sweet and well mannered because of Denis's training.

It was not snowing, but it was very cold. We went to the middle of a forest. I ran and ran with Denis's dog. I had fur-lined mittens; the other girls had fur coats, but I did not. They did not run with the dog. They stood near the fire, stomping their feet to keep from getting cold. I played with Denis's dog, and because I was always running with the dog and wearing fur-lined mittens, I did not have to stomp my feet to keep warm.

There were fifteen of us, and we all had a good time near the fire in the middle of the Russian forest.

Finally, we went home and drank good, Russian black tea. To make Russian tea, the leaves are put into the teapot and covered with boiling water. You cover the teapot with a kitchen towel to help the steeping process.

Then there is the sugar, which was in cubes at that time. I liked my cup of tea with two sugar cubes. Those were wonderful times and I will never forget them.

Chapter 5

Denis found me an apartment on the outskirts of Moscow It was located in a factory section. I had to walk twenty minutes to the get the subway to my new job.

Denis found me a translating job with the most popular journalist in Russia at that time. He was also on the *60 Minutes* television program every now and then. He was very nice to me and did not care when I got to work or what time I left. That was the old Russian way.

But the apartment building was practically vacant, as the surrounding factories had closed down. I was alone. Denis finally found me a new apartment and took me out of there.

One cold winter evening everything was ice. I finally made it to my apartment, and the radio was on. You could not turn it off or on; it just was on.

This was reminiscent of the Soviet times. There were radios in apartments that just turned on and off; you could not change the station. These radios were practically in every Soviet "new" apartment in Moscow. These apartments were for the middle class, factory workers, and KGB workers. Other apartments, such as Denis's, did not have a radio. They were too old.

What district one lived in depended on his or her job. For example, Denis lived in the "sports" district.

In my two-room apartment, I started to eat cake for dinner. It was the only thing I could afford on my pay. It was delicious with wafers and icing.

The grocery store was on the way to my apartment. At that time, grocery stores were practically just a whole in the wall of an old stone building. You had to pay for what you wanted before you picked it up. Every person behind the counter had to see your purchase ticket. Only then would they give you what you bought.

The apartment was sparse. The living room had a rug and sofa. It also served as the bedroom. Russians often slept on sofas because of a lack of room. The kitchen was bare but functional. I always went to bed with the radio drifting in my head.

Then Denis told me he found me another apartment and wanted me to pack. He did not like the life I was living. I was glad, as the apartment I was in was really in the middle of nowhere.

Chapter 6

The new apartment was in the center of Moscow and very pretty. It had hardwood floors and an aquarium with beautiful fish. It was a one-room apartment with a large kitchen. There was a wonderful samovar (an old Russian tea-making urn) on an old table by the window. I loved it there. And the rent was twenty dollars a month.

That still left me with ten dollars a month for food and clothing. Food was priced in kopecks (penny), and clothes were not much more.

Then Denis found me a new job. It was perfect for me.

My first real boss, who Denis found for me, was the top journalist in Russia. He was also a part-time journalist for the *60 Minutes* program in the United States. I would be his English language editor.

Through his father, Denis had high connections in the Russian government. He also gave this journalist tennis lessons. You see, sports people were not entirely forgotten by Yelstin's new government.

Denis did not introduce me to my new boss. He told me the address and said I should arrive at ten o'clock. Russians in those days slept late.

I was good at my job, and the journalist invited me everywhere. I went to his telecasting. I edited letters and journalistic work. He was always so nice. I never met his wife and children. But I did hear quite a bit about them, as he was a devoted husband and father.

Later, just before I left Russia, he died in a plane crash. Many said it was not an accident. His wife was left alone with the children.

Although I loved my work, I was very unhappy because I was alone. No one spoke to me, and I just came and went. Then it was my birthday. Denis came over on my birthday. When he saw how I was living, he told me to pack and move back home with him immediately.

At that time, I was seeing Gene, a very wealthy American businessman, and would come home late. I often bought fruit and a whole bottle of cherry liqueur for me after Gene dropped me off. Yes, I would drink the whole thing.

Chapter 7

Denis's friend Michael (Misha) stood tall, strong, and young. He had light brown hair and green eyes. He smiled a lot. He was there when I first moved to Russia. We became friends through many conversations and then became girlfriend and boyfriend.

We moved into an apartment his grandmother had owned. It was a "dual-dwelling apartment." There were many of those in the day. This meant two residents lived in the same flat. We were not that happy.

For dinner, we often ate pelmeni (Russian dumplings filled with various meats). Or we ate sturgeon, packaged six whole fish in a large, round, flat can. We ate it with potatoes. It was very good.

"Here is what we need," Misha said. We were on a street market, not far from his grandmother's flat. "We will have sweet, jarred peas, kvass, and volva tonight. Kvass is a fermented, nonalcoholic drink made from barley. Volva is a dried white fish. It is very salty, which is why he bought the kvass. This was a treat.

We slept together in a single bed. "Kira, wake up," he said. It was time for breakfast. The normal Russian breakfast included cured meats, black Russian rye bread (which you cannot buy anywhere but in Russia), and tea. There were no eggs, toast, or bacon.

We ate. He left with barely a word. I started to get ready for the day. I was not working at the time.

Misha taught me many things, including how to shop at a street market and how to eat something besides apples, bread, and eggs.

The street market, even near train stations, was mostly made up of *babushkas* (Grandmothers) selling food. They were decent and nice; they just needed the money. I did respect them but wondered where their families were. In Russia, multiple generations of the family lived together.

Eventually, Misha and I parted, but we remained friends. In later years, after I left Russia, I found out he had begun to work for a firm in the stock market. He was very level-headed and resourceful, indeed.

Chapter 8

I went to a press conference at which my boss was the main speaker. Many were there. That is when I met my future long-term boss. He was American, tall, and had dark blond hair and green eyes. His stature could fill a room, and he had no shame.

He came up to me and bluntly asked, "What do you do and for whom do you work?" I answered. He proceeded to ask me if I wanted to work for him. He was an American with money, so I immediately said yes.

I then had a new life. He seemed like a superman in the flesh. He was very important. And he had high connections—although not high enough, I would later find out.

He stayed to himself but mingled with many of the business elite. I started my job, writing in his hotel room. He wanted me to be his PR person, but I refused. I knew I could not, for example, write a press release.

Our relationship grew, and soon we would make love. Then I decided it was over. I moved downstairs to his office in the hotel. Everything was fine after that.

I met Lana, his secretary. She was thirty-five years old and had dark blond, shoulder-length hair. She was the perfect secretary. She always came to work on time and wrote the most beautiful—if I may say so—letters of correspondence from our boss. Lana always had a quick smile to come on her face.

"Good morning, Kirichka. How are you doing?" Lana would ask when I started my workday, which was usually about ten o'clock in the morning but sometimes not until noon.

We would talk. "What are you going to do today?" she would ask.

"I will write," I responded.

She often told me the news concerning the office. I was glad to hear it. We eventually became friends. When she left to work as a secretary for a Russian banker, things in the office turned dangerous.

My boss found me a special desk. It had a dark green leather top and a dark green, leather studded chair. He put it in the room next to his office room. I began to write.

At first, I wrote for the *World Trade Center Journal*. Through the years, I always added his name to mine on whatever I wrote. It was because of him that I could write; he financed me. He would pay me a monthly wage and provide me with all that was needed to write, including a computer, printer, fax, and endless long distance telephone service.

In months, I progressed to the most prestigious Russian and European journals and newspapers. It was not the money but the clout. My boss was grateful, because it would help him for years.

Chapter 9

My work would eventually take me to a town in lower Siberia. The town was called Ekaterinburg (Katherine's town). It was where the tsar's family was sent during the revolution and killed and buried.

I went to a big dinner. The mayor of the town sat at the head of the table, and I sat next to the deputy mayor. The deputy mayor was a true Russian from Siberia. He was stout and had a beard.

As we ate, we talked and laughed. During the "hot course," the deputy mayor asked me, "So, Kirichka, do you know how to make proper—not Russian—Siberian pelmeni (Russian dumplings filled with three different kinds of meat).

I answered, "Yes, of course!" You see, all Russian girls had to know how to cook. It was part of their pride. I said, "You take three different kinds of meats: cow meat, veal meat, and lamb meat."

He threw back his head and laughed. "No, Kirichka. For proper Siberian pelmeni, you use three different kinds of bear: a black one, a brown one, and a white one!" Everyone at the long table laughed. It is really Russian humor: he was just joking.

What I remember the most was getting ice cream blocks for dinner. Russian ice cream is so creamy and rich. I really do think Russian ice cream is the best in the world. For dinner, I would buy six small ice cream blocks from a kiosk not far from my hotel. They put them in a bag for me, and I would bring them up to my hotel room. It was, of course, vanilla ice cream; that is all they had then.

Sometimes I had a can of natural beef meat for dinner. It had to be opened, and as they did not have twist or electric can openers in Siberia at that time, I had to do it by hand. The meat was good and gave me strength. But I do still have a scar on my finger from opening one of those cans.

Actually, as history goes—or at least Russian lore—those cans of natural beef meat were why the Russians were able to defeat the Germans during the Nazi revolution. The beef is really strength-providing.

While in Ekathithrug, I walked to the top of the mound where the tsar and his family were buried. There was nothing to mark the graves. But it was calm, despite being in the middle of the city, and no one was there. The white winter sky touched the snow on the ground. In a way, it was very tragic.

After a few days, I returned to Moscow. I came back on the Russian Aeroflot plane with many interviews to show my boss and to turn into newspaper articles.

Chapter 10

Svetlana (Sveta) and I were taking the subway to work. We worked in the same office. She had moved offices to the upper floor of the hotel. Traveling together was convenient, as Sveta and I were best friends.

On the subway, no one talked. It was so quiet, and many were reading books. Although no one talked, they looked at each other with stony gazes.

Sveta stood, holding to the top railing. She was quiet and beautiful; no one could come close to her beauty. I carried a certain amount of pride. At least I knew I was pretty.

Sveta asked me, "*Zeitchick moy* [my little baby rabbit], are you cold?"

I replied, "No, I am not. Not at all." I wore a full-length, Russian cat fur coat. Sveta did not have a fur. I knew she was cold, but she did have a wool coat, although wool is not warm enough for the Russian winters.

We did not really do much of anything at work, but I continued to write. The simple truth was the boss liked pretty girls around him. During the winter high-couture fashion shows, Sveta was a catwalk model. She was very tall and skinny, with shoulder-length brown hair and brown eyes that contained a quiet calm.

At that time, only pretty girls got jobs and wealthy boyfriends. Everything was a big show. Others were married to men who were lazy, sometimes alcoholic. In any case, they could not hold a job or at least find one provided enough of an income to support a wife and family. Thus, those wives had to work.

One day there was a big meeting. None of his employees knew what it was about or with whom. We were supposed to serve coffee and tea. The boss was so happy with our service he actually talked about giving us a raise.

Our workday started at 10:00 in the morning and finished at 4:00, so we were very lucky girls indeed.

When my boss finally allowed, I hired two college students to help with the research I needed for my writing. My boss loved having them there, as he was very fond of young, energetic people. I was only twenty-two at the time.

They helped me a great deal. They went to the library for information, and they spoke with my contacts in the statistics department of Moscow. I spoke and read Russian but not well enough to converse in logistics.

"Kira Nikolaivna, what should we do today?" I let them talk in the early morning workday. Then I would ask them to do different tasks: call the statistics department and have them fax me certain facts, and go to the library (where only students, actually, were allowed) for other statistical information.

During my actual interviews, my boss sometimes provided an interpreter for me.

That was my job, and it continued for five years—until everything changed.

Sveta and I continued to be friends for years. We spent numerous hours at each other's flat. We talked, ate crepes with cut apples inside, listened to Frank Sinatra, and drank wine. She even taught me how to smoke, something most people did at that time.

Chapter 11

"Sveta," I said, "Dima never comes home until late;"

"That is the Russian man," she replied. "They leave their wives to work, take care of the house, cook dinner, and wait for them."

I would cry every night on the telephone with Sveta about Dima. She would always say, "He is no good for you!" But I loved him in a strange way and could not let go.

Dima and I, however, did go to Sveta's apartment many times to spend an evening with her. We brought fruit, vegetables, and meat. Those were things she could not afford. Sveta often made chicken soup for her dinner, because it was cheap. At work, I was paid like an American, but the other Russian girls were paid like Russians, which was not very much.

Often, when we went over, she would make blinis with apples inside. It was delicious, and Dima would eat two or three of them.

Afterward, we went for walks in the evening. It was dark and wintertime, and the snow glistened underneath the moon. We would talk and laugh. We had been drinking Georgian wine. It was the only wine to be found in Russia, except for homemade berry wine. The wine was good and kept us warm during our walks.

In general, Americans in Russia did not have these experiences or joys. They mostly ate at the few restaurants Moscow had and went to an Irish bar, which was on Novee Arbat (New Arbat) Street.

Russians never went to restaurants. They considered their home meals to be better. They would invite guests over, and the meal would last for hours and include vodka and wine.

Sveta and I stopped talking to or seeing each other after three years of being best friends. Things changed when she married and became pregnant. She then met only with women who also had babies. I was not yet married or had a baby. We finally lost each other. She moved; I moved. It was a very sad ending, as we used to be so happy together.

Chapter 12

It was Friday, and I was getting ready to go on a date. His name was Gene, and he was millionaire. He had dark blond curly hair and was an old-school Italian. In those days, I would usually drink a glass of champagne while I got ready.

In those days, American businessmen flocked to Russia. It was thought that there was much money to be made, but that was wrong. And where large sums of money could be made, there were usually strings attached.

We had just met. I was sitting in lounge of the hotel where I worked and, I learned, he was staying. I was drinking a glass of champagne after work. He just came up to me and started talking.

We would always at meet in the hotel lounge at seven o'clock. He would take me to dinner, and we would talk for hours. Then it progressed.

He started asking me to come to dinner engagements and business meetings. I enjoyed all of it. These were not ordinary. There were private dinners in the basement of one of the most prestigious museums in the country. Steaks were served that filled the huge dinner plate. Everyone drank Georgian wine, and many toasts were made.

There were dinners in buildings with no outdoor indications they were restaurants. You had to have contacts to even know they existed, let alone dine there. Red velvet chairs sat around the tables. They served a full seven-course dinner.

Then there was the Chinese restaurant. All the mafia went there. You could pretty much do as you pleased. There were long tables with tablecloths. Twelve or more people could eat at one of those tables. The lights were low and the service impeccable.

This was an elite life, and money was no object. Gene was quite at home in this lifestyle. You see, he came from Italian Mafia and led a similar life.

Then there were the business meetings. They met in offices located in hotels. Everything and everyone were so quiet, except you could hear the fax machine; there was no scanning then. The meetings ran about an hour. Only half an hour was spent on business, while the rest of the time, they exchanged stories.

Gene bought me a high-fashion dress and shoes. The dress was black. It fell to the floor and had a slight slit at the bust area. It was beautiful. "I like these shoes," he said. They were suede, with chain around the ankles. The tailors would adjust the clothes on the spot. This was just to be with him and his various partners. Beauty had to be complete, and that included being adorned in the latest fashion. Girls were not out for true love but financial stability.

This continued throughout the winter and then he went back to New York. He came back two months later. I found out he was married with a newborn. He offered me a chalet in Nice, France, but I refused.

He had spent nearly two million dollars "investors"—the Mafia—just confiscated. He had been told he would get double back. Then it ended.

I never saw or heard of him again.

Chapter 13

Finally, I began to write for publications. I had written for the *World Trade Center Journal* for a while. Then I began writing for other prestigious publications, including the top political/business newspaper in Europe and the top newspaper in Russia. Meetings with high government officials and high-ranking business executives secured my employment.

I worked day and night. I decided I needed better clothes to wear to interviews, so I hired a seamstress. They made very pretty clothes, but my income did not allow for high fashion, which was everywhere.

During this time, I was seeing Dimitri (Dima). He was tall, and his father had worked for the KGB. He drove people around, like a taxi. There was no taxi service in Moscow. People would just drive, and people would just hail them from the streets.

I met Dima in the hotel where I worked. He was a guard for the hotel. He was a year younger than I. When I learned this, I knew deep down it would not last. But he really did fall in love with me.

I would make us a dinner of fish, salad, and potatoes. He grew to his full strength with my dinners. We even had his mother and her husband over for supper. I made a gingerbread cake with jam inside (*pryanik*).

Dima and I made a life together. His mother complained he should not have to pay part of the rent, as he had a home with her. That changed, because I believed he should pay all the rent as long as we were together (I have always been old-fashioned). She finally agreed.

Dima started to go to college with my encouragement. He hated it. Then he found a job.

It was Christmas Eve, and he had just begun to drive. He would pick up anyone who needed a taxi. He found many, and he made quite a bit of money. Then he picked up the person who would be his future boss.

Chapter 14

Dima's future boss was a Russian money-market player. His wife worked for Russia's Finance Department. He knew many high authorities and was very smart, having the equivalent to a master's degree.

Dima's boss drank alcohol at the end of the day. In those days, most of the real business happened at night. And Dima, because of his boss's wishes, drank with him.

Dima and I had the perfect apartment and the perfect life. I will always love that apartment. It was near a market that sold clothes, which I bought. I had two mohair sweaters, which were very warm and pretty. I bought a pair of patent leather flat shoes, which I wore every day.

After shopping, I would go for a walk in the park, which was only a couple blocks away from the outside shopping area. The park was natural; nothing had been done to what naturally grew there. There were people walking their dogs, people jogging, and couples just sitting on the benches. I was so happy.

I would wake up in the morning to sunshine. Dima and I would have tea and talk. Life could not have been more perfect.

Early in the summer, Dima and I drove from Moscow to St. Petersburg. It was a beautiful drive. The straight road was lined with fir trees. I can just imagine the tsars driving along that road.

After three hours, we arrived at our destination. He showed me where his mother went to college. Then he took me to Catherine the Great's home.

The land was filled with so many fountains! They were everywhere. We walked through the grounds, and I was amazed. It was so beautiful. Dima took me to the dock, where Catherine the Great would go as a little girl.

We stayed in a hotel. It was very clean and private. It was situated by the water and was two hundred years old.

We ate our breakfast of a glass of sour cream with sugar and buckwheat kasha. And, of course, strong tea. Then we were on our way.

We went to a restaurant in the back of a beautiful orchard adorned with lattices. Dima took many pictures. We were very happy.

Dima quit college to work full time with his new boss as his bodyguard and driver. His boss grew to rely on Dima for moral support, among other things. He paid for Dima's gym membership, and they exercised together. He also took Dima on trips to his dentist in Italy. I never went with them, until we all went to Finland together.

Dima's boss hired half of a Russian train. The train was of the old-world style. There were beds in the compartments and small tables with tablecloths. One was supposed drink the tea and eat the meals they served. However, his boss brought food from the elite grocery store in Moscow. We sat in several compartments, eating and drinking.

The guests were bankers and bodyguards, and a few close friends. We had such good meals. It was easy to fall asleep until we arrived in Finland.

In Finland, Dima's boss had reserved a whole hotel for a big banquet and party. It was New Year's Eve, which is a very celebrated holiday in Russia.

Everyone got ready for the banquet. Some took a steam in the steam room. Others went to the tanning beds. I took a steam and a tan, as Dima had

wanted me to, so I would look my best for the banquet. He had bought me a two thousand dollar white dress and said I looked like the *sneg princessa,* a snow queen from a Russian old fairy tale.

The banquet was long with many toasts. Everyone was serious and boisterous at the same time. We ate a lot and then it was time to go to the attached veranda to see the fireworks Dima's boss had ordered. In Russia, on New Year's Eve—as everywhere else it seems—there are always fireworks on that holiday.

As I had a little too much to drink and was very tired, I went to the restroom, because I was not feeling so well. I missed the beginning of the new year. That was the beginning of the end of Dima's and my relationship. According to Russian superstition, it is bad luck for a couple not to be together when the clock turns 12:01 a.m.

Dima could not forgive me, and we just went to bed. On the train that night, he slept in the lower bed of the bunk bed and I slept on the top. We had been together for three years, but I knew it would soon be the end for us.

We returned to our apartment in Moscow. I cooked his dinners as usual, and he still worked for his boss. He worked long hours: 7:00 a.m. to midnight. I always waited up for him, so we could spend time together, and he would tell me about his day.

Then he started bringing home a bottle of whiskey, which he would drink in one sitting. I did not say anything. We were over at his mother and stepfather's apartment for dinner one evening, and while we were smoking in the kitchen, his mother told me I better do something, or he would leave me. She said she thought it might be over between Dima and me unless I did something. I told her I felt it was already over, and there was nothing I could do. He was just moving on.

Two months later, Dima moved back into his mother's apartment and his old bedroom. He met a girl he picked up from the bus stop. I know, because he would still call and come to see me after work. One day, I just said good-bye. Everyone had earlier thought we would soon to be married.

We saw each other before I left Russia. I gave him the Christmas decorations he had bought for our Christmas tree. The decorations cost $600.00, and they sang when plugged in. They were Walt Disney characters. They would pop out of their houses and sing famous American Christmas carols. I thought it would be good for his future children. And after all, considering what he had done for me, I felt he should have them.

Dima thanked me, and we said good-bye. I was going back to the United States. Dima mentioned I was really skinny, which was the look those days in Russia, and I just smiled. Our good-bye was good, and I was glad it happened that way.

During this period, the coup was beginning. Conservatives (still Communist) and the Democrats were fighting in the parliament. The parliament then, during this fight, was something Yeltsin wanted to dissolve.

However, Barnnikov in the KGB was "Yeltsin's ear." The KGB gathered intelligence and other facts for Yeltsin. The KGB was on Yeltsin's side.

Chapter 15

I continued to write and work for the same boss. Sometimes I was paid, and sometimes I was not, except for the rubles and dollars I received for my articles, as I had become a noted freelance journalist.

Then I had my girlfriends. One of them was the daughter of the Russian finance minister. Another was a daughter of a very rich businessman in Moscow. He owned the most popular nightclub, where everyone who was anyone went.

Young dancing girls were popular parts of the nightclubs. They danced to loud techno music, which was popular music among young people. They were clothed, of course; it was not a striptease. Young businessmen would sit in booths—which were expensive to get—and watch the girls dance.

It was popular for the elite young people to drink tequila. We would lick between the thumb and the finger and then pour then salt on it. We would drink a whole shot, lick the salt, and finish by biting into a lime slice.

My girlfriends often went to parties on the outskirts of Moscow. I was never invited. I was not that important among the young Russian elite.

I will always remember a party at a different nightclub. It played the popular techno music, but it had a fountain and green grass outside with lights. It was beautiful.

My boss had opened a business with Russian partners. He had the best clientele and was making a lot of money. That is when the terror happened.

When the business became successful, his partners wanted to take it over. The Russian partners brought in the county Mafia to persuade my boss to sell his business to them. But he was fearless and only encouraged by the money he was making in his own business.

He had to hire bodyguards. Eventually, because of the threats, he could not leave his hotel room. I often saw him there, in the same hotel room where I started to work for him, eating hot pot soup and taking baths. He could not go anywhere.

One day, he got a telephone call that promised him money to buy out the partners. He went to the subway, as the partners had cut him off from most of his share of money, and when he entered the subway, he was shot twenty-one times in the head and neck. His bodyguards had done nothing. He had owed the bodyguard firm money, so that was not surprising.

The day it happened, I received a phone call from the mother of one of the girls who worked for him. She told me the news. I was in shock. Until I left Moscow, I often walked by the bullet marks in that subway station.

That night, I saw his body on the news. They even showed the bullet holes in his head. I was scared. Then I remembered that in the hotel elevator one day, one of Mafia said to me, "We are only after him, not you."

I knew nothing about the money. At the end, he was not paying me regularly. And he allowed none of us in his office.

I went to the hospital the next day for a scheduled surgery. I stayed there a week. In the meantime, police locked the office where I had worked.

Even though we had stopped seeing each for months by then, Dima came to stay with me for a month, because I was scared. He had heard the news.

I went to the funeral. A newspaper photographer took my picture, but it was never published.

Only later would that time haunt me.

Chapter 16

The coup happened in August 1992. It started with the conservatives. They were not pleased with Yeltsin's reforms. But really, it was in progress during the past several years about which I have written.

The common people were not really affected. It is true: there was always bread and food. It was all political. Yeltsin had given up the Ukraine and allowed the everyday Russian to become a businessman without being tied to the Mafia.

The Mafia did exist, and strongly. In Moscow, in Siberia, where there was no law. The mayor of the town was a small dictator.

And there was the parliament, which blocked all of Yeltsin's reforms. They were the conservatives.

Yeltsin "tamed" the KGB. They were Yeltsin's "ear." He and the KGB were criticized by the conservatives in the parliament. But the KGB would also later be reformed.

Chapter 17

Yelstin was in the White House, and the first floor was burning. All of us girls were at work. Many went home, but I did not.

Yeltsin urged parliament to reform. But they were conservatives and wanted Yeltsin out. He proceeded to dissolve the parliament. That was the beginning the coup.

Foreigners in the hotel were watching CNN on the television in the hotel lounge. I did not join them.

I ran to that bridge and hid under it, because a few snipers were on the hotel roof. The hotel was only several blocks from the White House.

My previous boss, who would later be murdered, actually went into the White House and let Yelstin use his cellular phone. The coup had destroyed all phone lines and power in the White House.

My boss was inside the White House, and I was drinking vodka with four Russian men underneath a stone bridge. But at least I was not alone.

The men were factory workers. They had just gotten off work and gone to the area of the coup. Their clothes were drab. They were good people, and none of what was happening affected them. They finally went home, as did I.

Demonstrators accused deputies in the Russian parliament of blocking all reform. Konstantin Truyestsev, a leader of the democratic movement, was vital during the coup. Many people followed him. Yeltsin was approved and secured by the Russian people.

A few people, however, wanted a return to communism. "It was an easier life," they said. These were mostly people in the lower middle class. Many of them had become entrepreneurs during the Yeltsin period.

The next day, the coup was over. Yeltsin had succeeded.

It was Yeltsin versus the communists in court. Shakhrai, the presidential adviser, announced he was stepping down from government to serve as Yeltsin's private lawyer. Shakhrai resigned on May 6, 1992.

Shakhrai represented Yeltsin before the highest courts in Russia. The court investigated the legality of Yeltsin's decree to dissolve parliament in November 1992, three months after the coup attempt by Kremlin hard-liners, banning all activities of the Soviet Communist Party.

Chapter 18

Everyone I knew, meaning Russians, went on normally during and after the coup as normal. It did not affect them; they only talked about who would be the victor. In Russia, the people accommodate any leadership. It is something that must be understood.

Russian people are good and just want their own lives. In general, they are not ambitious, as they were beaten down for so many years. But that changed under Yeltsin. And although there was the Mafia, most average Russians could become entrepreneurs.

I remember meeting a man who owned his own business, selling washers and dryers. Before then, everyone washed their clothes by hand in the bathtub. They used a very strong bar of soap that was very hard and abrasive. His business made a fortune. He was not in any trouble with the government or Mafia; both were the same in the city of Moscow.

I also met a man who graduated from Harvard with a degree in business. He worked for a foreign bank in Moscow and was also unaffected by the coup. Soon, I would teach his child English.

Chapter 19

It was the end. After my boss was killed, I spent a month recovering, barely going outside my apartment. But in order to pay rent, I needed a job.

I started teaching English to Russian businessmen and children. It was hard work, as I usually had to go to their offices or homes, even in winter. Sometimes they came to me. I had recently moved to an apartment, where I rented a room. It was on the most famous street in the middle on Moscow: Starry Arbat.

I made enough to survive. And then I made enough to be able to buy some things now and then.

I had a favorite student. His name was Ivan, and he was twelve years old. He was the son of the banker. He did his homework and in six months was speaking English. They took him to the United States. When they came back, they told me he was able to converse in English with children his own age. I was very happy.

Ivan and I would watch the movie *Star Wars* and sometimes go to one of the Moscow McDonald's. I would, of course, speak only English to him, with a little translation into Russian if he did not understand.

I lost touch with that family, as well as my other students, when I left Russia. It is sad.

Chapter 20

It all began in an apartment located near the train to the subway. It was about twenty-minute subway ride east of Moscow, and it was very cold in the winter. There was ice on the ground and freezing snow in the wind. There were barely any trees.

The snow fell and the wind howled. I learned to face this with my head held high, like all the Russians there did.

I worked for the top journalist of the country at that time. I was paid twenty-five dollars a month. My apartment rent was twenty dollars a month. I lived on dark, Russian rye bread and apples. When I saved a little, I bought eggs.

I was told how to pick red berries off the trees to make preserves. The berries were there for the birds during the winter.

I was also told how to make buckwheat kasha (*meele*). It was very delicious and nutritious. You just simmer it for ten minutes, and it is done! You can add sunflower oil and mushrooms, if you want, or just eat it plain with salt.

I lived in silence next to an apple orchard, which I used to walk through frequently. When I was hungry, I pick an apple for a snack and nourishment. It was very juicy and sweet and sour at the same time. They are called

Alexandravnaya apples. I will never forget apples on rye bread with red berry preserves.

The coup was stirring, but in Russia, at least for the common Russian, life is always a quiet calm.

Epilogue

How did I eat and keep clean? It was the open market located less than a block from every apartment complex. There were wide areas of flowers and trees to walk through to get to the open market.

There, babushkas sold the crop from their country dachas. There was a lot to choose from; parsley, dill, potatoes, tomatoes, cucumbers, radishes, beets, carrots, and even turnips. This was all Russian cuisine fare. But this was the summertime.

In the winter, there were only root vegetables and potatoes. But the babushkas were there all the same. In the winter, they would stand there, bundled in wool scarves and thick wool coats.

I bought many vegetables, fruits, and flowers. Only the local outside stores sold red meat and fish. There were flies everywhere. The stores had mostly "blocks of meat," not a particular cut. And the fish was mostly carp.

Inside stores sold also the basics: Russian salami, provolone, and sausage cheese, which is similar to Gouda but made with sausage drippings and smoked.

As for milk, you brought your own jar to the milk trucks that came by, and they filled it. The milk was untouched and delicious.

These stores and open markets were nestled among trees. They were also nestled among wildflowers, daffodils, and lilacs in the spring. It was wonderful and beautiful.

I often went to the kiosk or bread store to buy *lapooshka,* a sweet, rye, round biscuit. I would eat them in the blistering snow, and they would keep me warm. I would also buy Russian dark rye bread. I also bought chocolates and put them in my pocket to eat on the way to the subway, as all Russian children do. That also kept me warm.

To keep clean, I bathed and showered. Soap in Russia is awfully strong and dry. I purchased it at the local Apteka (drugstore), which was also near every apartment complex.

One day, when I had a little bit of extra money, I bought a turkey leg. It was huge. And while I boiled it, the bone stuck out of the pot. I had turkey for three days in my first apartment, thirty minutes by subway from the heart of Moscow.

Russia is really a magical place, with fir trees in the winter and the low white sky touching the snow-covered ground. In spring, the daffodils are everywhere, and lilacs give off their sweet scent. In summer, birch trees sparkle in the sun. And in the forest during autumn, mushrooms are plentiful for the babushkas to pick for a good mushroom soup. It is a simple and happy life.

If only I were in Russia again.

About the Author

Kira von Korff grew up in a Russian household. During childhood, she lived in both the United States and Russia. Her family is from pre-revolutionary Russia.

She went to Stanford and the private liberal arts school, The Colorado College. She studied political philosophy and ballet. Dance led her to Russia at sixteen when she performed ballet there. She would return later, at twenty-one, to write columns for prestigious publications, such as the *Wall Street Journal Europe*, *Finance News* (the leading Russian newspaper), and the *World Trade Center Journal*.

Kira von Korff is a Russian Baroness from years ago in Russian history. Her great-grandfather was a Baron and a General in the last Russian tsar's army. His portrait hangs in the Hermitage in St. Petersburg today.

She now resides in the country in Maine with her husband.

Printed in the United States
By Bookmasters